S0-AFD-178

QUABOAG REGIONAL H.S.
LIBRARY/MEDIA CENTER
284 Old West Brookfield Rd.
Warren, MA 01083

CRITICAL THINKING
— IN —
AMERICAN HISTORY™

Results of the American Revolution

Summarizing Information

Colleen Adams

The Rosen Publishing Group, Inc., New York

Thanks to Mr. M for sharing his knowledge and love of American history.

Published in 2006 by The Rosen Publishing Group, Inc.
29 East 21st Street, New York, NY 10010

Copyright © 2006 by The Rosen Publishing Group, Inc.

First Edition

All rights reserved. No part of this book may be reproduced in any form without permission in writing from the publisher, except by a reviewer.

Library of Congress Cataloging-in-Publication Data

Adams, Colleen.
Results of the American Revolution: summarizing information/
Colleen Adams.—1st ed.
    p. cm.—(Critical thinking in American history)
 Includes index.
ISBN 1-4042-0417-2 (library binding)
1. United States—History—Revolution, 1775–1783—Juvenile literature.
2. United States—History—Confederation, 1783–1789—Juvenile literature.
3. United States—History—Revolution, 1775–1783—Study and teaching
(Secondary)—Juvenile literature. 4. United States—History—Confederation,
1783–1789—Study and teaching (Secondary)—Juvenile literature.
I. Title. II. Series.
E208.A325 2006
973.3—dc22

                                                                2005001396

Manufactured in the United States of America

On the cover: At left: A print published in 1860 entitled *General George Washington Receiving a Salute on the Field of Trenton, 1776*. At right: American Revolutionary soldiers fighting in the Battle of Guilford Court House, North Carolina, March 15, 1781.

Contents

The Struggle for Independence

By the 1760s, more than a million people had settled in the thirteen colonies along the eastern coast of what would later become the United States. Although England gained control of North America when the French and Indian War ended in 1763, the cost of winning was great. In the process, England had spread its wealth and resources thin. The British government decided that colonists should help repay its financial debt in return for England's military protection of the colonies. The colonists, who had before enjoyed great freedom, rebelled by boycotting British imports and staging protests. In 1775, Americans' fight for independence from England finally resulted in the Revolutionary War, which ended in a victory for the United States in 1783. The work of rebuilding the economy, paying off war debts, restoring farms, and restructuring the laws of the government were just a few of the challenges Americans faced.

Q & A

✓ What did England gain as a result of the French and Indian War?

✓ How do you think that England forced Americans to help pay for the costs of the war?

✓ What struggles did Americans face after winning the Revolutionary War?

✓ List several causes of the American Revolution and then list its effects.

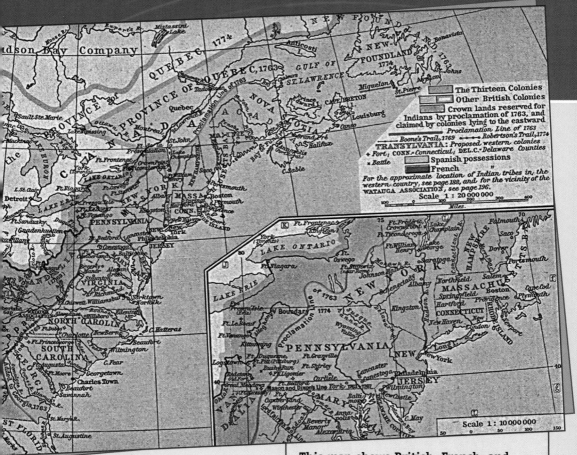

This map shows British, French, and Spanish colonial possessions between 1763 and 1775. Native Americans still controlled land beyond the Appalachian Mountains, but even after the Proclamation of 1763 was issued by the British, colonists still pushed farther west.

After the war, many Native Americans who fought on the British side were left without their British allies or the land they were promised. Americans who had remained loyal to the British had their land and possessions taken and were driven out of America. Many African Americans who had fought in the war for independence were not recognized as free citizens. Examining the causes and effects of the American Revolution can help us to understand how this war changed history.

The Sugar Act and the Stamp Act

When England won the French and Indian War in 1763, the colonists were well established. They made their own laws and paid taxes within the colonies to support themselves. All of this changed in 1764, when England passed the Sugar Act ordering colonists to pay additional taxes on imported items such as sugar and molasses. Many colonists did not want to pay the new taxes. The following year, British parliament issued the Stamp Act. All printed materials such as newspapers, pamphlets, and legal documents were stamped requiring colonists to pay taxes on each item. England said the tax money collected would be used to "defend, protect, and secure the colonies." Many colonists felt that this practice was unfair and called it "taxation without representation." The colonists were angry. They did not want to pay taxes to a government that did not offer them a chance to participate in making its laws.

Paper Work

Pretend you are a colonist living in Boston in 1765. Write a letter to a local newspaper that explains your outrage at Parliament's demands for higher taxes. Address the following questions in your letter:

✓ How have the higher taxes affected you and your family?

✓ What do you think would happen if England continued to charge colonists high taxes?

A. Bobbett sc   Darley

The Stamp Act (1765) was created to help England pay off its war debts, but the law was immediately protested by colonists, as depicted in this drawing. One possible reason why there was so much resistance to the law was because it affected elite colonists and businessmen who felt the tax undeservingly reduced their profits.

Colonists believed the new taxes were enacted to control them and take away their independence. Many colonial merchants did not think they could afford to run businesses when taxes were being placed on everyday items such as newspapers, tea, and sugar.

The Boston Massacre

By 1768, the relationship between colonists and the British had worsened. Many colonists protested the British government and its new tax policies. British soldiers were sent to Boston to maintain order. Colonists refused to listen to British soldiers and often responded by calling them names and spitting at them. On March 5, 1770, British soldiers tried to unsuccessfully control a crowd that threw rocks at them. British soldiers led by

Fact Finders

There were many causes that led to the deaths of five people in the Boston Massacre. Choose the statements below that name causes of the Boston Massacre:

a. Many colonists were angry about the presence of British soldiers stationed in Boston.

b. The colonists threw cargoes of tea brought in by British ships into Boston Harbor.

c. A large crowd of colonists yelled and threw snowballs and rocks at British soldiers.

d. Many colonists believed the British government was taxing them unfairly.

Tell a friend about the causes you chose and why you chose them. Explain the effects of each cause.

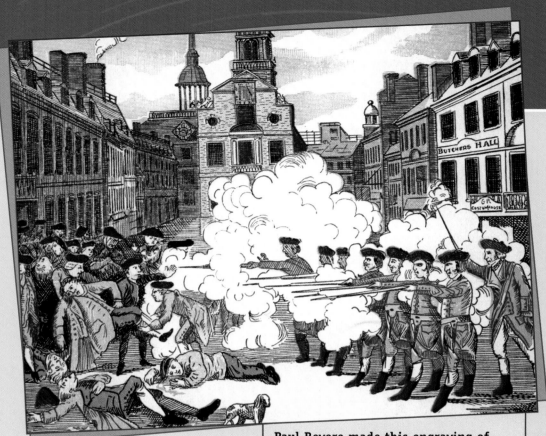

Captain Thomas Preston
were sent in to control the
angry crowd. Preston

Paul Revere made this engraving of the Boston Massacre shortly after its occurrence. In order to reach all the colonists, many of whom were illiterate, Revere expressed his outrage visually.

ordered his troops not to fire. No one is sure what happened next, but it's possible that someone in the crowd yelled, "Fire." Within moments, British soldiers fired on the crowd, killing four people. A fifth person died later and another six were wounded. The most well-known colonist who lost his life that day was Crispus Attucks, an African American sailor. Preston was tried for murder of the colonists and later acquitted of the charges. Two of his soldiers were convicted of manslaughter but were later pardoned.

The Boston Tea Party

The Tea Act, passed in 1773, made the East India Company the only company who was selling tea in the colonies. The colonists protested by boycotting the tea and refusing to unload it from British ships when they reached colonial ports. The first efforts to unite the colonies against British control were made by independent groups such as the Sons of Liberty. The Sons of Liberty was a secret organization of merchants, artisans, and tradesmen that formed in Boston in 1765 to protest the Stamp Act. Members of the group often wrote newspaper articles and participated in protests to speak out against the actions of the British government. The Sons of Liberty organized the Boston Tea Party as a way of showing their disagreement over the tea tax imposed by England. On December 16, 1773, 200 men dressed as Mohawk

Q & A

✓ What did the act of dumping tea into Boston Harbor symbolize for the colonists?

✓ Why do you think the Sons of Liberty chose to protest in this way?

✓ What other ways could the colonists have chosen to protest high taxes?

✓ How would you protest a law that you thought was unfair?

In this image, colonists along the shore watch as Sons of Liberty members disguised as Mohawk Indians toss 342 chests of British tea into Boston Harbor in protest of the Tea Act. British parliament was equally outraged at the protest and immediately closed Boston Harbor and enacted the first of several laws known as the Intolerable Acts.

Indians marched onto three British ships and dumped their cargo into Boston Harbor. Sons of Liberty groups in other seaports such as Maryland, New York, and New Jersey later staged similar protests.

The Intolerable Acts

When the British learned about the Boston Tea Party, they immediately passed five laws directly affecting the colonists in Massachusetts. The colonists referred to these laws as the Intolerable Acts. The Boston Port Act ordered the port of Boston closed until Boston paid for the destroyed tea. The Massachusetts Government Act removed elected council members and replaced them with members chosen by the king. The Administration of Justice Act ordered British officials accused of committing crimes in the colonies to go to England for trial. The Quartering Act allowed British troops to remain in houses within the colonies if no barracks were available.

Fact Finders

Event: Boston Tea Party

Who: Sons of Liberty

Where: Boston Harbor

Why: To protest taxes

When: December 16, 1773

How: Members of Sons of Liberty, dressed as Mohawk Indians, dumped tea into Boston Harbor.

Significance: The Sons of Liberty made a symbolic protest against the high tax and communicated that they wanted it repealed.

What was one of the main causes that led to the Boston Tea Party? What were two of the effects of the Boston Tea Party?

Patrick Henry, a colonial lawyer and accomplished public speaker, is pictured speaking to delegates at the First Continental Congress in Philadelphia on September 5, 1774. At the meeting, the colonists drafted a plan to resist laws enacted by British parliament and adopt a Declaration of Rights and Grievances.

In 1774, delegates from the colonies formed the First Continental Congress and met to discuss a course of action to protest the Intolerable Acts. They passed a resolution to support Massachusetts in its fight against British control. The delegates agreed to boycott all goods imported from England until the Intolerable Acts were repealed. It was suggested that each colony organize and train its own militia in order to prepare for the possibility of war.

Battles of Lexington and Concord

On April 19, 1775, British troops led by General Thomas Gage headed toward Concord, near Boston, to destroy guns and ammunition stored by the colonists. When patriots learned of British plans to invade Concord, Paul Revere, William Dawes, and Samuel Prescott were sent to alert the minutemen. Paul Revere hung two lanterns in the Old North Church steeple in Boston as a signal that the British were crossing the Charles River. There were seventy-five minutemen led by Captain Jonas Parker waiting for British troops at Lexington Green. When the British troops led by Major John Pitcairn arrived, shots were fired, killing several Americans. Parker finally ordered

Word Works

✓ **militia:** A group of trained men who are not soldiers but who can serve as members of the military in an emergency.

✓ **minutemen:** American soldiers of the Revolutionary War who were ready to fight at a "minute's warning."

✓ How are the meanings of the words "militia" and "minutemen" the same? How are they different?

Artist Franklin McMahon created this image of the meeting of British redcoats and colonial minutemen at the Old North Bridge in Concord on April 19, 1775. American minutemen outnumbered British soldiers in the engagement, and British troops quickly retreated to Boston after suffering casualties of nearly 300.

his men to withdraw, knowing that they were outnumbered.

Parker and seven other colonists were killed. While the British marched into Concord, units of colonial militia fired on them continuously. Colonial militia later surrounded the city of Boston beginning the American Revolutionary War.

Battle of Bunker Hill

During the first year of the war, much of the fighting took place around Boston where British troops were stationed. Colonial militia surrounded the city and prevented the British from expanding its control. On June 16, 1775, Colonel William Prescott led 1,200 minutemen up Bunker Hill to Breed Hill across the river from Boston Harbor. The next day, General William Howe marched British troops up the hill to attack the patriots. The Americans fired on the British and twice forced them back. On the third attack, the British won the battle by taking both Breed Hill and Bunker Hill. The patriots fought hard against British troops but were eventually forced to retreat. The Battle of Bunker Hill was the bloodiest conflict in the Revolutionary War, and the war's first major engagement. Even though Americans were forced to retreat, they showed the British that they were strong and able fighters. General George Washington, commander in chief of the

Q & A

✓ What assumption did the British make about the Continental army and its ability to take Bunker Hill? Explain why you think the British made this prediction.

✓ What did the Continental army prove to the British during the Battle of Bunker Hill?

✓ How were the soldiers in the Continental army different from the soldiers in the British army?

Continental army, reached Boston shortly after the battle. He trained ordinary colonists to become soldiers by teaching them

Just months after the battles of Lexington and Concord, the patriots faced one of the most difficult conflicts in the entire Revolutionary War—the Battle of Bunker Hill—which took place in Massachusetts on June 17, 1775. Patriot forces were forced into retreat after running out of gunpowder, and the British soon took control of the area, though their casualties were also severe.

both the strategy of war and about their weapons. He also taught them how to work together.

Declaration of Independence

Shortly after the battles of Lexington and Concord, colonial representatives met at the Second Continental Congress in 1775. After hours of debating, they decided to make one last appeal to England. In a statement called the Olive Branch Petition, the delegates proclaimed their loyalty to their mother country and asked King George III to repeal the Intolerable Acts. When the king refused, Congress made the decision to declare independence.

On June 7, 1776, the Second Continental Congress appointed a committee to write a formal declaration explaining why the colonies wanted complete freedom. Thomas Jefferson was asked to write the initial draft. Committee members including Benjamin Franklin and John Adams made suggestions about how to revise the document. The Declaration of Independence included a preamble and three main parts. The preamble explained why the document was written. The first section stated that all people are equal and have

Think Tank

✓ Organize a small group of classmates into four teams.

✓ Assign each team one of the parts of the Declaration of Independence.

✓ Assign roles within each team, such as reader, writer, and researcher.

✓ Use classroom sources such as the dictionary, encyclopedia, and the Internet to aid research.

✓ Teach other groups important facts about the part you researched in the Declaration of Independence.

Within days of declaring the colonies independent of England, members of the Continental Congress, including Thomas Jefferson, Benjamin Franklin, and John Adams, adopted the Declaration of Independence on July 4, 1776.

the right to life, liberty, and the pursuit of happiness. It also stated that when a government tries to take these rights away, the people have the right to form a new governing body. The second section listed the grievances against England and the steps taken by the colonies to settle their differences. The last section stated that the thirteen colonies declared themselves free and independent. The declaration was approved and signed by Congress on July 4, 1776, seven years before the war ended.

The Battle of Saratoga

In 1777, British general John Burgoyne planned to lead troops from Canada to Albany. He believed that if the British could take control of the Hudson River region, they could successfully separate New England from the other colonies and win the war. The plan was to keep Washington's army from getting the supplies and reinforcements it needed from New England. Burgoyne set out to take over Albany from New York City. Although he captured Fort Ticonderoga along the way, his plan was foiled when three British armies coming from different directions failed to meet him. Instead, Burgoyne's army of 7,000 soldiers tried to carry out the plan alone and fought against American forces at the Battle of Oriskany and the Battle of Bennington. In both incidents, the British were forced to retreat.

During the third battle, the Battle of Saratoga, Burgoyne and his men surrendered to patriot forces on October 17, 1777. This battle was a major victory for the Americans and a turning point in the war.

Get Graphic

✓ Take a look at the map showing the routes of the British troops.

✓ On the map locate the following: a) St. Leger's route; b) Albany; c) Saratoga; d) Hudson River.

✓ Do you think that Burgoyne's plan would have worked if his replacements had met him as planned? Why or why not?

20

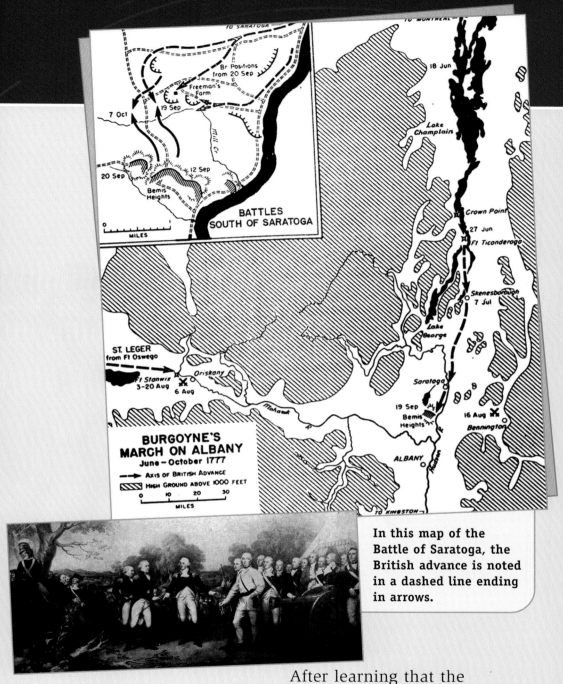

In this map of the Battle of Saratoga, the British advance is noted in a dashed line ending in arrows.

After learning that the Continental army could not support itself, France offered money, supplies, and troops to help the Americans.

Siege of Yorktown

In 1778, the location of the war shifted and many battles were fought in the South. British general Charles Cornwallis moved his troops out of South Carolina in the spring of 1781, planning to take control of Virginia and cut off southern supply routes. He stopped in Yorktown to wait for British troops, but French ships instead blocked the harbor. At the same time, American forces led by General Washington and French troops led by General Rochambeau attacked on land.

Without supplies or a way to escape by land or sea, Cornwallis fought for several weeks knowing he could not win. He and his army of less than 8,000 men finally surrendered on October 19, 1781. This battle signaled the end of the American Revolutionary War. The United States and England began peace talks in 1782.

Paper Work

Imagine you are General Cornwallis in the final days before your surrender on October 19, 1781. Write a journal entry from two perspectives:

✓ Personal: Introduce yourself and explain your military responsibilities and accomplishments during the American Revolutionary War.

✓ Descriptive: Describe what the engagement is like and your feelings as the Americans close in and French troops arrive by sea.

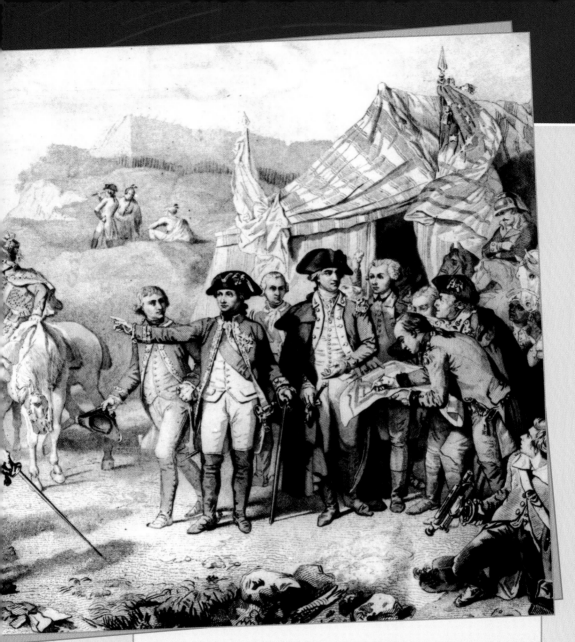

The Revolutionary War ended when British troops surrendered at Yorktown, Virginia, in 1781. Americans defeated the British with the help of French naval forces, and after General George Washington ordered Marquis de Lafayette to trap British troops in Virginia. In this image, Washington and Lafayette give the last orders for the attack at Yorktown.

The Treaty of Paris

The last shot of the Revolutionary War was fired in Yorktown in 1781. The war did not officially end, however, until the Treaty of Paris was signed on September 3, 1783. After more than a year of talks, England and the United States compromised with each other. The Treaty of Paris named the United States as a free nation and established its borders from the Great Lakes in the north to Florida in the south, and from the Atlantic Ocean to the Mississippi River. According to the terms of the treaty, England agreed to take all of its troops out of America and the United States agreed to pay all debts it owed England.

Fact Finders

What were the two most important provisions of the Treaty of Paris (1783) for the United States?

a) The treaty recognized the United States as an independent country and established its boundaries.

b) The treaty protected Indian land and kept colonists from settling west of the Appalachian Mountains.

c) The treaty forced France to support the United States in the American Revolutionary War.

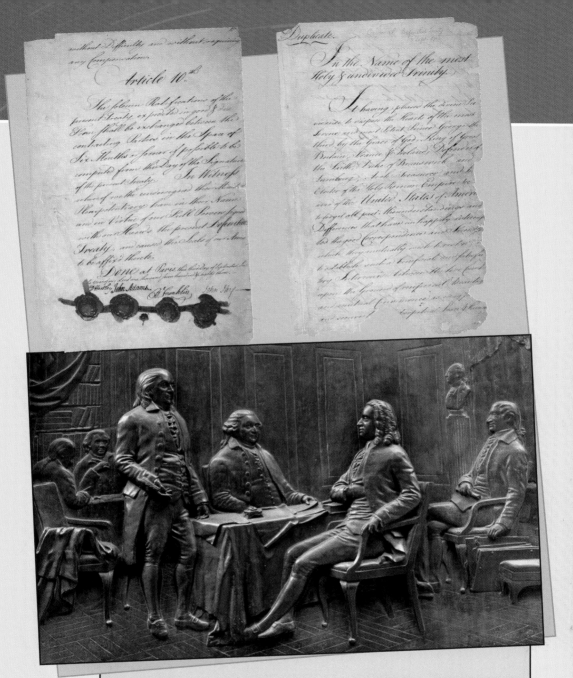

The Treaty of Paris is pictured above a relief sculpture of Benjamin Franklin signing the historic agreement that officially ended the American Revolutionary War in 1783. This sculpture is located at Old City Hall in Boston, Massachusetts.

Social Effects of War

When the war ended, not all Americans were satisfied with the results. Some were left without a home while others struggled to win their freedom. When the fighting during the war moved west into Indian land, both the British and the Americans tried to win Native American support. England convinced the majority of Native Americans to fight on its side, promising them that it would protect their land. When the war ended, Native Americans lost their British allies and the land for which they had fought. As American settlers eventually moved farther and farther west, Native Americans were unable to retain land that was rightfully theirs.

American Loyalists supported the British government during the American Revolution. They wanted to

Word Works

✓ **Loyalist:** People in the colonies who remained loyal to England during the American Revolution.

✓ **ally:** A group or country that has joined with another for a particular purpose.

Write a summary statement about this chapter using these two words.

find peaceful ways of protesting higher taxes and did not believe that colonists should go to war. During the conflict, many Loyalists had their property and land taken away. By 1782, 100,000 Loyalists left America. Many moved to England, Canada, and British colonies in the West Indies.

Many of the Loyalists who sided with England were Native Americans who feared losing their land. This is Joseph Brant, a Mohawk chief who was educated by the British and remained faithful to them throughout many conflicts, including the the American Revolutionary War.

African Americans were also faced with difficult choices during the American Revolution. Many chose to fight on the side of the British because they were promised their freedom. As many as 5,000 others chose to fight on the American side. Even though the issue of slavery was debated when the Constitution was drafted in 1787, slavery was not made illegal.

A Weakened Economy

After the war, the United States owed England millions of dollars in war debt. According to the Articles of Confederation, Congress did not have the power to tax citizens, so there was no way to get the money to repay the debts. When Congress asked the states for money, they often refused because there were no laws demanding they contribute funds. The paper money Congress had issued during the conflict was of no value after the war because it was not backed by gold or silver. Each state now printed its own money, which

Paper Work

✓ How did the laws written in the Articles of Confederation contribute to the financial problems many Americans faced after the Revolutionary War?

✓ Think about what you know about the Articles of Confederation. (Look the document up online, http://www.usconstitution. net/articles.html). Think about how the farmers' financial problems were related to the way the government was structured. Write one paragraph explaining the problems and another paragraph explaining how these issues may have been caused by the way the Articles of Confederation was structured. Discuss your opinions with the class.

Among the economic problems faced by the colonists before and after the Revolutionary War were discrepancies in currency between the thirteen colonies, which made trade between them more difficult. These are examples of colonial coin and paper currency.

complicated commerce and trade between states.

By 1786, Americans were also feeling the effects of a depressed economy. Perhaps the hardest hit were farmers who had borrowed money to pay for equipment that was in high demand during the war. After the war, when the demand decreased, they had a difficult time repaying their debts. Farmers had to deal with creditors, taxes, and the risk of losing their farms. These debts caused farmers financial stress and uncertainty about their futures.

Shays's Rebellion

After the war, farmers in the thirteen original states were feeling the effects of poor harvests, economic depression, and high taxes. Many were in danger of losing their farms or had already lost them. Some were put in jail because they couldn't repay their debts. In 1786, farmers in Massachusetts asked their state government to provide paper currency to stop the foreclosure of their homes and to stop sending farmers to jail for their debts. When there was no action taken, Daniel Shays, a former officer in the Continental army, led a group of Massachusetts farmers in armed protests that lasted for months. The group rebelled by forcing state courts to stop hearings that were making judgments about farmers' debts. Shays's group hoped to prevent further trials and imprisonment of poor farmers.

When Shays's men tried to attack a federal arsenal in Springfield, troops of more than 4,000 men led by General William Shepard were sent to stop the uprising. The group largely fled the area, ending the rebellion. Shays and the other leaders were eventually

Paper Work

Imagine that you are a farmer living in Massachusetts in 1786. Write a letter to a friend explaining two events that caused you to lose your farm and two ways it has affected you and your family.

30

In 1787, Daniel Shays led a rebellion of poor Massachusetts farmers who rejected high taxes and low wages. The mob succeeded in keeping Northampton courts closed, the event that is re-created in this image.

pardoned. Due to this rebellion and similar uprisings in other states, American leaders realized that the Articles of Confederation no longer served the needs of the people. They believed they needed a more unified system of government for the United States.

The Articles of Confederation

The Articles of Confederation were submitted to the Second Continental Congress on July 12, 1776, shortly after the Declaration of Independence was signed. The articles represented the first agreement made between the thirteen American states. Created during the war, its theme reflected that a strong national government with too much power could be dangerous. For this reason, colonial leaders gave the states more decision-making control. After Shays's Rebellion, however, Americans realized that Congress was severely limited in its powers. Congress could not raise money by collecting taxes, for example, and it had no control over interstate or international trade. Congress could pass laws, but it could not force the states to follow them. If Congress needed to

Think Tank

Divide the classroom into two sides: one group that supports a strong central government and another that wants to give more power to individual states.

✓ Each side should use classroom resources to prepare an argument defending its position. Both groups should debate their opinions with information backed by facts.

raise money, for instance, it could request it from the states, but the states did not have to obey. The government was forced to request that individual states enforce laws on their own.

Many states refused to cooperate with the federal government. When state representatives met in 1787 to make changes to the articles, they realized that major changes were needed to provide a more balanced distribution of power between state and federal governments.

The Articles of Confederation was America's first constitution, written while the war was still in progress in 1776 and 1777. After uprisings in several states, however, lawmakers were forced to consider a stronger Constitution.

The Constitutional Convention

The Constitutional Convention opened on May 25, 1787, to revise the Articles of Confederation. There were fifty-five delegates in attendance, including Benjamin Franklin, George Washington, and Alexander Hamilton. It didn't take long for the delegates to realize they needed a new constitution for the United States. James Madison and Edmund Randolph from Virginia drafted a proposal called the Virginia Plan. The basis for this proposal was a strong national government with three branches: a legislative branch, an executive branch, and a judicial branch. According to the plan there would be two houses. Members of the House of Representatives would be elected by popular vote. Seats in this lower house would be given to each state according to its population. Members of the Senate would be chosen by state legislatures. Each state would have two senators.

The delegates originally disagreed about the amount of representatives each state should have but were convinced by Roger Sherman of Connecticut to

Q & A

✓ Why do you think delegates from the Southern states wanted slavery to remain legal?

✓ How do you think the use of slaves contributed to our nation's economy and overall wealth?

✓ How many years would pass before slavery became illegal in America?

Helen Clark Chandler created this painting of the signing of the Constitution by thirty-nine members of the Constitutional Congress on September 17, 1787. Most of the signing members were elite colonial figures who owned property and had slaves.

compromise and adopt the plan. The delegates also disagreed and argued over the issue of slavery. The Northern states wanted slavery to be banned, but the Southern states wanted to keep slavery. A compromise was finally reached. The Northern side agreed that Congress could not make slavery illegal for twenty years. Finally, the discussions ended. The Constitution was signed by the delegates on September 17, 1787 and ratified by the states on June 21, 1788.

Three Branches of Government

The Constitution has been written to provide a set of laws and principles that safeguard the rights of Americans. It sets specific criteria for dividing the responsibilities of both the state and federal governments. The Constitution outlines a democratic system in which there is a "separation of powers" between three branches of the federal government.

The legislative branch, which is represented by Congress, has the power to make laws. The executive branch, which is represented by the president and his advisers, has the power to enforce laws. The judicial branch, which is represented by the Supreme Court and other federal courts, has the power to interpret laws.

Under the rules of the Constitution, the people elect their own leaders for a specified amount of time. Those elected leaders have the right to make changes or amendments to the Constitution if the majority of the people agree to change it. Even though the Constitution was

Think Tank

✓ Choose two partners. Each person in the trio should be assigned one of the branches of government: legislative, executive, or judicial.

✓ Each group should write five questions about each branch.

✓ Each student should conduct research and answer questions about each branch.

✓ Each person should then present a short explanation of one of the three branches.

written more than 200 years ago, it is a "living" document that continues to provide Americans with modern laws.

After months of debate, and several drafts, the Constitution of the United States was finished in September 1787, and ready to be ratified. The new Constitution was challenged by America's citizenry and the document was printed in newspapers throughout the thirteen states for review. In 1788, the Constitution was approved.

The Bill of Rights

Many delegates thought there needed to be some guarantee that Americans would always have their individual rights protected by the government. Congress added ten amendments, called the Bill of Rights, to the Constitution on December 15, 1791. These ten amendments include the following rights: freedom of speech, freedom of the press, freedom of religion, and freedom of assembly. Some amendments were also included to protect Americans from unreasonable searches and seizures of their homes and personal property, from cruel and unusual punishment, and to guarantee the accused the right to a fair and speedy trial.

By 1791, Americans had come a long way since the days of paying high taxes on sugar and tea. They had stood up for themselves when they believed they were taxed unfairly. They demanded to have a voice in the decisions made by their government. When their rights were taken from them, colonists fought bravely in the Revolutionary War. Documents such as the Declaration of

Word Works

✓ **amendment:** An official change made to a bill, law, or other document.

✓ **assembly:** A group of people gathered together usually for a specific purpose.

The suffix "-ment" means the result of an action.

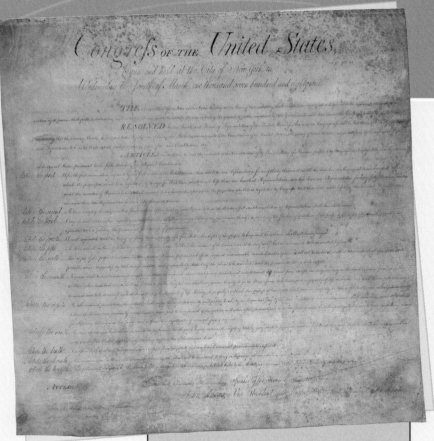

Americans resisted the Constitution because it contained no references to individual rights. This problem was remedied by the Bill of Rights, seen here, which was drafted in 1791 by James Madison

Independence, which asserted America's independence from England, and the Articles of Confederation, which established the first national government, helped make the United States a new nation. Lessons learned from the experiences of war and its aftermath helped Americans define the principles and values of the American people. The United States Constitution and the Bill of Rights continue to balance the rights and responsibilities of state and national governments and their citizens.

Timeline

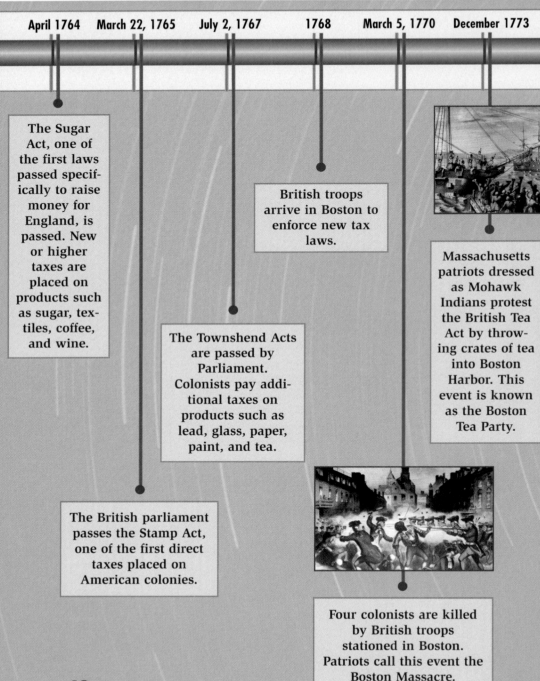

April 1764   March 22, 1765   July 2, 1767   1768   March 5, 1770   December 1773

The Sugar Act, one of the first laws passed specifically to raise money for England, is passed. New or higher taxes are placed on products such as sugar, textiles, coffee, and wine.

British troops arrive in Boston to enforce new tax laws.

Massachusetts patriots dressed as Mohawk Indians protest the British Tea Act by throwing crates of tea into Boston Harbor. This event is known as the Boston Tea Party.

The Townshend Acts are passed by Parliament. Colonists pay additional taxes on products such as lead, glass, paper, paint, and tea.

The British parliament passes the Stamp Act, one of the first direct taxes placed on American colonies.

Four colonists are killed by British troops stationed in Boston. Patriots call this event the Boston Massacre.

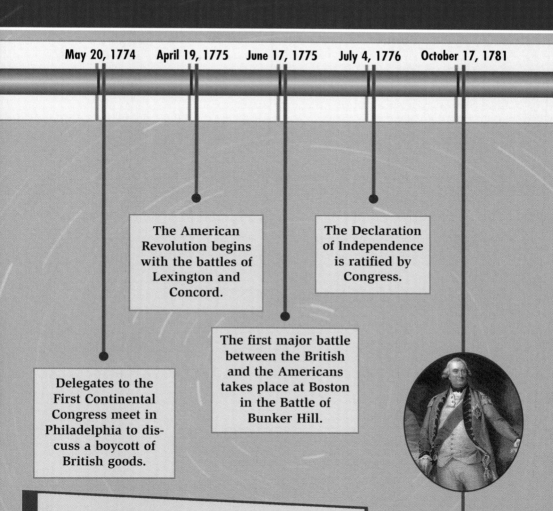

May 20, 1774   **April 19, 1775**   **June 17, 1775**   **July 4, 1776**   **October 17, 1781**

The American Revolution begins with the battles of Lexington and Concord.

The Declaration of Independence is ratified by Congress.

The first major battle between the British and the Americans takes place at Boston in the Battle of Bunker Hill.

Delegates to the First Continental Congress meet in Philadelphia to discuss a boycott of British goods.

Get Graphic

✓ This timeline presents information about events during the American Revolution. Use it as a model to help you create a timeline of the battles of the American Revolution. Use information from this book and do additional research if needed.

British general Cornwallis surrenders at Yorktown. The American Revolutionary War ends.

Graphic Organizers in Action

Get Graphic

Study these examples of graphic organizers. They organize information about events during the American Revolution.

✓ Can you create a cause and effect chart about the Boston Tea Party?

✓ Can you create a KWL (What I **Know**, What I **Want** to Know, What I've **Learned**) chart about how life in the colonies changed after America won the Revolution?

Cause and Effect Chart

CAUSES

England passes the Sugar Act in 1764 to help raise money to pay war debts.

England passes the Stamp Act in 1765, requiring colonists to pay taxes on printed papers.

The Boston Massacre takes place in 1770. Five colonists are killed by British soldiers.

Members of the Sons of Liberty dress as Native Americans and throw tons of tea into Boston Harbor as a protest against taxes on tea in 1773.

Parliament passes the Intolerable Acts in 1774. These laws anger colonists and unite them against British rule.

EFFECT

The battles of Lexington and Concord start the American Revolutionary War in April 1775.

K W L Chart

What I Know	What I Want to Know	What I've Learned
✓ The colonists disagreed with England's decision to charge them higher taxes. ✓ The Declaration of Independence was passed on July 4, 1776. ✓ There were problems with the economy after the war that the government was unable to address.	✓ Which key events led to the start of the American Revolution in 1775? ✓ Why did colonial leaders feel it was important to write the Declaration of Independence during the American Revolution? ✓ What events resulting from the war caused leaders to con-sider changing the structure of the American government?	✓ Colonists protested several laws, such as the Sugar Act (1764), and the Stamp Act (1765), that placed taxes on goods in the colonies. Other events such as the Boston Massacre and the Boston Tea Party increased hostility on both sides. ✓ The Declaration of Independence was written to proclaim the thirteen colonies as free and independent states that would no longer be ruled by England. ✓ A new set of laws written in the Constitution of the United States was passed in 1788 to create a unified system of government that balanced power between three main branches.

Venn Diagram

Native Americans

✓ Had to give up their land to western settlers

✓ Lost support of British allies that promised to protect their land

✓ Lost their land

Loyalists

✓ Lost their home and possessions

✓ Many left America during and after the war

✓ Were resented by many patriots

Glossary

acquit (ah-KWIT) To declare a person free of wrong-doing, as in the case of a previous accusation.

allies (AL-lyz) Groups such as countries associated or united with another in a common purpose.

ammunition (am-yoo-NISH-un) The objects fired from any weapon, or material that can be exploded. Bullets, bombs, and gunpowder are types of ammunition.

artisan (AR-tih-san) A person who works at a trade requiring skills with his or her hands.

barracks (BEHR-aks) A building or group of build-ings in which soldiers live.

boycott (BOY-kot) To join with others in refusing to deal with someone (as a person, organization, or country) usually to show disapproval or to force acceptance of terms.

compromise (KAHM-pro-myz) An agreement over a dispute reached by each side changing or giving up some demands.

declaration (deh-kla-RAY-shun) To announce in a formal way.

draft (DRAFT) To compose a written document.

grievance (GREE-vants) A complaint about something.

legislature (LEH-jis-lay-chur) A body of people that has the power to make, change, or cancel laws.

militia (mil-ISH-uh) A body of citizens having some military training but called into service only in emergencies.

pardon (PAR-duhn) To release a person from further punishment.

parliament (PAR-luh-mint) An assembly that is the highest legislative body of a country.

preamble (PREE-am-bul) An introduction to a law or constitution that often gives reasons for the parts that follow.

ratify (RA-tih-fy) To give legal approval in a group vote.

repeal (ree-PEEL) To do away with or officially cancel.

Web Sites

Due to the changing nature of Internet links, the Rosen Publishing Group, Inc., has developed an online list of Web sites related to the subject of this book. This site is updated regularly. Please use this link to access the list.

http://www.rosenlinks.com/ctah/rear

For Further Reading

Beller, Susan Provost. *Revolutionary War*. New York, NY: Benchmark Books, 2003.

Bobrick, Benson. *Fight for Freedom: The American Revolutionary War*. New York, NY: Simon and Schuster, 2004.

Herbert, Janis. *The American Revolution for Kids: A History with 21 Activities*. Chicago, IL: Chicago Review Press, 2002.

Masoff, Joy. *American Revolution, 1700–1800: Chronicle of America*. New York, NY: Scholastic, 2000.

Moore, Kay. *If You Lived at the Time of the American Revolution*. New York, NY: Scholastic, 1998.

Nardo, Don, ed. *The American Revolution*. San Diego, CA: Lucent Books/Thomas Gale, 2003.

Osborne, Mary Pope, et al. *The American Revolution: A Companion to Revolutionary War on Wednesday*. New York, NY: Random House, 2004.

Index

A

Adams, John, 18
Administration of Justice Act, 12
African Americans, 5, 9, 27
American Revolution/Revolutionary
    War, 4, 5, 15, 16, 22, 24, 26, 27, 38
Articles of Confederation, 28, 31,
    32–33, 34, 39
Attucks, Crispus, 9

B

Bill of Rights, 38, 39
Boston Massacre, 8–9
Boston Port Act, 12
Boston Tea Party, 10–11, 12
Bunker Hill, Battle of, 16
Burgoyne, John, 20

C

Constitution, U.S., 27, 35, 36–37, 38, 39
Constitutional Convention, 34
Continental army, 17, 21, 30
Continental Congress, 13, 18, 32
Cornwallis, Charles, 22

D

Dawes, William, 14
Declaration of Independence, 18–19,
    32, 38–39

E

economy, U.S., 28–29

F

Franklin, Benjamin, 18, 34
French and Indian War, 4, 6

G

Gage, Thomas, 14
George III, King, 18

government, branches of, 34, 36–37

H

Hamilton, Alexander, 34
House of Representatives, 34
Howe, William, 16

I

Intolerable Acts, 12, 13

J

Jefferson, Thomas, 18

L

Lexington and Concord, battles of,
    14, 18
Loyalists, 26–27

M

Madison, James, 34
Massachusetts Government Act, 12
minutemen, 14, 16

N

Native Americans/Indians, 4, 5, 26

O

Olive Branch Petition, 18

P

Parker, Jonas, 14–15
Parliament, 6
Pitcairn, John, 14
Prescott, Samuel, 14
Prescott, William, 16
Preston, Thomas, 9

Q

Quartering Act, 12

About the Author

Colleen Adams is a writer and editor of children's history books. She lives with her family in Lockport, New York.

Photo Credits: Cover (left and right), pp. 21 (bottom), 25 (top), 29, 33, 35, 37, 39, 40 (top and bottom), 41 © National Archives and Records Administration, Washington, DC; pp. 4–5 © Perry-Castañeda Library Map Collection/Historical Maps of the Americas/The University of Texas at Austin; pp. 7, 9, 10–11, 13, 16–17, 21 (top), 31 © Bettmann/Corbis; p. 15 © Franklin McMahon/Corbis; p. 19 © PoodlesRock/Corbis; pp. 22–23 © Hulton Archive/Getty Images; p. 25 (bottom) © Kevin Fleming/Corbis; p. 27 © MPI/Getty Images.

Designer: Nelson Sá; Editor: Joann Jovinelly; Photo Researcher: Nelson Sá